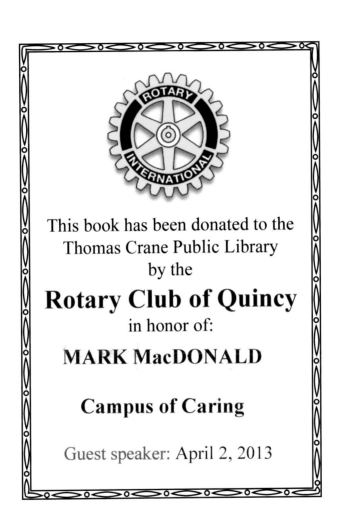

This book has been donated to the
Thomas Crane Public Library
by the

Rotary Club of Quincy

in honor of:

MARK MacDONALD

Campus of Caring

Guest speaker: April 2, 2013

Published in 2014 by The Rosen Publishing Group, Inc.
29 East 21st Street, New York, NY 10010

Photo Credits: Key tl=top left; tr=top right; cl=center left; c=center; cr=center right; bl=bottom left; bc=bottom center; br=bottom right; bg=background

CBT = Corbis; iS = istockphoto.com; SH = Shutterstock; TF = Topfoto

8bc iS; 18tr SH; 22br, tr CBT; bl, cr TF; 23bg TF; 25tr iS; 26bc, c, cl SH; 27t, tl iS; br, br SH; 29c iS

All illustrations copyright Weldon Owen Pty Ltd

Weldon Owen Pty Ltd
Managing Director: Kay Scarlett
Creative Director: Sue Burk
Publisher: Helen Bateman
Senior Vice President, International Sales: Stuart Laurence
Vice President Sales North America: Ellen Towell
Administration Manager, International Sales: Kristine Ravn

Library of Congress Cataloging-in-Publication Data

Einspruch, Andrew.
 Rain forest habitats / by Andrew Einspruch.
    pages cm. — (Discovery education: Habitats)
 Includes index.
 ISBN 978-1-4777-1324-2 (library binding) — ISBN 978-1-4777-1483-6 (pbk.) — ISBN 978-1-4777-1484-3 (6-pack)
 1. Rain forest ecology. 2. Habitat (Ecology) I. Title.
 QH541.5.R27E36 2014
 577.34—dc23
                         2012043614

Manufactured in the United States of America

CPSIA Compliance Information: Batch #S13PK3: For Further Information contact Rosen Publishing, New York, New York at 1-800-237-9932

Discovery
EDUCATION™

HABITATS

RAIN FOREST HABITATS

ANDREW EINSPRUCH

PowerKiDS press.

New York

Contents

What Is a Rain Forest?

Rain forests are dense forests usually found in wet, warm climates not far from the equator. They feature tall trees, a huge variety of plants and animals, and plenty of rain. They are perfect habitats for animals and plants, and are home to more species of life than anywhere else on Earth.

There are several kinds of rain forests. Tropical rain forests have high humidity, rain that falls evenly all year round, and no clear seasons. A monsoon rain forest has two seasons—wet and dry—and the trees are usually deciduous. Temperate rain forests are not as dense as other forests, and their trees are mostly evergreen. Rain forests are also found in different kinds of land areas. Some are in mountains, others valleys, and still others are found on flatlands.

Disappearing act

In 1800, rain forests covered 7.1 billion acres (3 billion ha) of the world. By 2009, it was only 3.5 billion acres (1.4 billion ha).

An alphabet soup of animals

Rain forests are home to many different life-forms, both big and small. They fly, slither, crawl, dig, and swim.

1. Anaconda
2. Anole lizard
3. Brazilian tapir
4. Bushmaster snake
5. Capybara
6. Cock-of-the-rock
7. Emerald tree boa
8. Geoffroy's spider monkey
9. Giant armadillo
10. Harpy eagle
11. Hoatzin
12. Jaguar
13. Kinkajou
14. Linne's two-toed sloth
15. Red howler monkeys
16. Reticulated poison dart frog
17. Silky (pygmy) anteater
18. Tamandua
19. Keel-billed toucans
20. Tree frog
21. Tree porcupine
22. Zebra butterfly

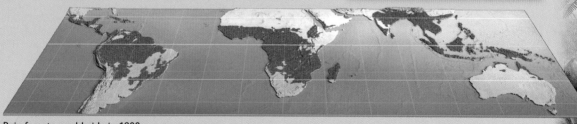

Rain forests worldwide in 1800

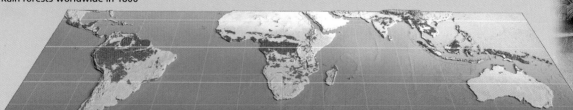

Rain forests worldwide in 2009

Different Layers

What a rain forest looks like depends on where you look. Life in the tops of the trees is very different from life far below. In a rain forest, the top layer is called the emergent layer. This is where the tallest trees stand above everything else. Their leaves are usually broad and waxy to withstand direct exposure to sun and wind.

Below the emergent layer is the canopy, formed by masses of large trees. Rain forest canopies are where the world's greatest diversity of plants and animals live. Below this layer is the understory, which gets limited sunlight. At the bottom is the rain forest floor, which is dark and damp because it gets almost no direct sunlight.

Kapok leaves

Vines

Banana leaves

Fungi

The emergent and canopy layers of the rain forest receive full sunlight, while the floor layer at the bottom gets almost none.

Emergent
This layer is made up of the tallest trees that poke out of the canopy, such as the kapok tree, which grows to 150 feet (46 m). Spaced far apart, these trees are home to high-flying eagles, butterflies, and some monkeys.

Canopy
This has the largest variety of plants and animals in the rain forest because there is so much sun and food. Many of the animals living there never set foot on the ground for their entire lives. Branches in the canopy are often covered with thick vines.

Varying heights

In the emergent layer, plants grow to between 100 and 240 feet (30–75 m). In the canopy, they grow to between 60 and 130 feet (18–40 m), and the understory has plants that grow up to 60 feet (18 m).

Understory
This layer receives little sunlight and is very humid, with minimal air flow. The plants here, such as the banana plant, tend to have large leaves to catch what little sun comes through.

Floor
The forest floor receives so little light that few plants can live there. It is mostly home to fungi, which live on dead plants and animals.

Did You Know?
From above, the canopy looks like a thick mass of trees, but the branches do not usually touch or overlap. They stay a few feet apart, which helps to protect them from diseases.

The Canopy

The rain forest canopy is home to a huge diversity of plants and animals. They thrive on the sunlight that reaches this layer and find food, water, and shelter among the leaves.

A common type of canopy plant is the epiphyte. Epiphytes grow from seeds that lodge in tree trunks or branches, and grow upon other plants like parasites. Unlike parasites, however, they do not take nutrients from the host tree itself. Instead, they get water from rain and the atmosphere and nutrients from a variety of sources, such as dead insects, animal droppings, dust, and debris that floats in the air.

TANGLE AND STRANGLE

The strangler fig is a type of epiphyte that starts life high in a host tree from a seed dropped by a bird. The fig's roots grow down the trunk to the soil below, eventually surrounding the tree in a woody "corset." This corset prevents the tree from growing outward, so it dies and rots, leaving the fig standing on its own.

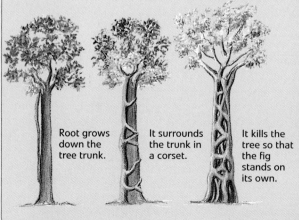

Root grows down the tree trunk.

It surrounds the trunk in a corset.

It kills the tree so that the fig stands on its own.

View from the top

Many animals in the rain forest enjoy this top-down view of their world. Up in the canopy, they eat leaves, seeds, fruits, and nectar.

Epiphytes

The ant plant is an epiphyte that provides a home for ants. In return, the ants supply it with nutrients in the form of dead insects and droppings.

Vines

Thick vines hang down from emergent trees and intertwine with canopy tree branches.

Bromeliads

These epiphytes can collect 2 gallons (8 l) of water a day. The water attracts animals and insects, which leave droppings that help feed the plant.

Towering trees

Emergent trees rise through the canopy to reach as high as 20-story buildings.

1 Howler monkey
2 Scarlet macaws
3 Spider monkey
4 Toucan
5 Resplendent quetzal

Ground Level

Termites
These insects eat bark and other plant litter. Their mounds are nutrient rich and are absorbed into the soil.

Dark, damp, and cool, the rain forest floor is a very different place from the canopy. The few plants that live there do not need much light and have very large leaves to capture the little bit of light that filters down.

The soil of the rain forest floor is naturally low in nutrients. But the floor is also covered in dead animal and plant material, which is broken down by insects, bacteria, and fungi to release nutrients into the soil. These nutrients are quickly absorbed by plant roots.

Food source
Insects help break down dead plant matter and also provide food for birds.

Dead and alive

This tree is dead but has life all over it. Fungi and bacteria break it down slowly, releasing nutrients from dead cells inside. Eventually the log will disintegrate, but the new plants it supports will take its place.

Decomposers
The many fungi on the rain forest floor help decay plant and animal waste.

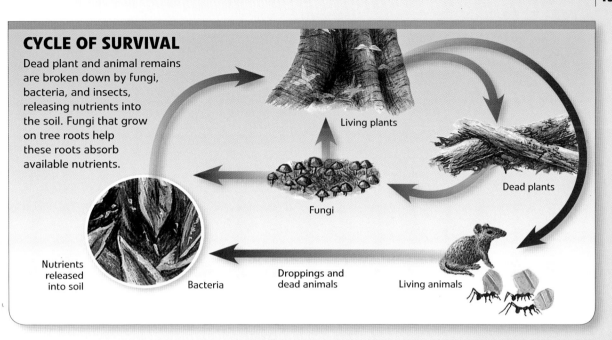

CYCLE OF SURVIVAL

Dead plant and animal remains are broken down by fungi, bacteria, and insects, releasing nutrients into the soil. Fungi that grow on tree roots help these roots absorb available nutrients.

Living plants

Dead plants

Fungi

Nutrients released into soil

Bacteria

Droppings and dead animals

Living animals

Quick to decay
Warm, humid, damp conditions speed the decay of dead plant and animal matter on the forest floor.

Vegetation
Because there is so little sunlight here, there is much less vegetation than one might expect.

Animal life
Animals crawling along the rain forest floor can find bark, seeds, wood, and leaves to eat.

Piggyback Plants

Little sunlight on the forest floor means plants have difficulty growing. Epiphytes are plants that solve this problem by growing on the branches of tall trees in the canopy or emergent layer. Their seeds germinate on branches or trunks, and they grow from there. Vines, ferns, and bromeliads all "piggyback" tall trees but usually do not hurt them.

Reaching for the sun

Vine species make their way toward sunlight in many ways. Their tendrils may hook on to the branch, coil around it, twine along it, or stick to it.

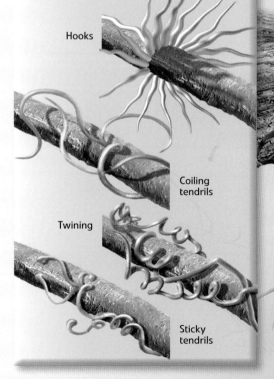

Hooks

Coiling tendrils

Twining

Sticky tendrils

Piggyback clusters
Different kinds of epiphytes can cluster together on the branches of canopy and emergent trees.

Water reservoir
The leaves of some bromeliads form a tank that holds water. Animals are attracted to this, drinking water or laying larvae there. Their debris and droppings become nutrients for the plant.

Mouse opossum
This mammal finds water to drink and insects to eat at the bromeliad reservoir.

Eyelash viper
Eyeing the mouse opossum, this viper looks for its next meal by the water.

ORCHIDS

One kind of epiphyte is the orchid, a familiar rain forest dweller. These plants have become popular with gardeners outside the rain forest because they can flower for half a year and are easy to care for.

Phalaenopsis orchid

Eggs and larvae
This mosquito uses a "raft" to lay her eggs on top of the water in the bromeliad. The water is also home to tadpoles and other insect larvae.

Birds

Rain forest canopies are home to some of the most interesting and varied birds in the world, producing a riot of shapes, sizes, and especially colors. And there are many of them—half of all bird species, including hawks, eagles, vultures, parrots, and owls, are found in the Amazon and Indonesian rain forests alone.

As is typical in bird species, male rain forest birds have more color and plumage than their female counterparts. The males display these assets to try to win the attention of a mate.

Crowning glory

Many rain forest birds have spectacular feathers, crests, and color patterns. The Victorian crowned pigeon has a colorful and stylish crest on top. The cock-of-the-rock has an unusually shaped, bright red crown, and the toucan has bright eye rings.

Scarlet macaws

These parrots make their home in the canopies of South America's rain forests. They live in flocks, can fly 35 miles per hour (56 km/h), and live for more than 50 years.

IN THE MIX

They say birds of a feather flock together. But this is not always so in tropical rain forests. Large groups of different species can flock together to feed on the abundant fruits and insects.

Cock-of-the-rock

Toco toucan

Victorian crowned pigeon

Attention seeker

The blue bird-of-paradise goes to great lengths to attract a mate. He hangs upside down, spreads his wings, fluffs his breast feathers, and makes a show of his two long, black tail plumes. The males gather in a group to see which can outdo the others.

Mammals

Rain forests are home to their fair share of mammals—vertebrate animals that, like humans, give birth to live offspring and suckle their young. Many mammals have evolved into excellent climbers so they can thrive in the branches of the canopy. The best climbers tend to be the smallest animals because they are the lightest ones.

Pygmy marmoset

Found in the Amazon, the pygmy marmoset is the world's smallest marmoset. Its head and body are only 6 inches (15 cm) long, but this more than doubles if the tail is added. Pygmy marmosets are active during the day and dine on insects, small animals, fruits, and tree sap.

Ocelot

Like other cat species, the ocelot is good at climbing, which helps it hunt for birds. The ocelot is known to sleep in the lower branches of trees.

Musky rat–kangaroo

The world's smallest kangaroo lives in the rain forests in northeast Australia. It actually bounds like a rabbit, rather than hops like a kangaroo. It is also unusual in that it has an opposable first toe, a feature that appears in other marsupials but not in other kangaroos.

Orangutan

This primate is the largest of the tree-dwelling mammals in the rain forest. Its size, however, makes it vulnerable to hunters because it is easily seen.

Tamandua

This anteater's tail is good for holding on to and climbing trees and for wrapping around branches for stability. Its wormlike tongue and sticky saliva enable it to eat insects, mainly ants and termites.

Sloth

This three-toed sloth has a greenish tinge due to algae that attach to its hairs. It is known for its slow movements and for going down to the ground only once a week to defecate. Its claws attach securely to the branch while it sleeps and may stay attached even after it dies.

Blue morpho

This butterfly's blue appearance comes from the tops of its wings, which reflect blue light. When not flying, it sits with its wings closed so it is less visible to predators.

Chameleon

The chameleon hides by changing its skin color to match its surroundings. It moves its eyes independently, seeing in all directions without moving its head.

Firefly

This insect produces light from its abdomen to attract a mate. The light blinks on and off. In certain parts of Thailand, fireflies sit in the mangroves and all blink in unison.

Sloth moth

The sloth moth lives on a sloth's shaggy coat. When a sloth reaches the forest floor, the female sloth moth lays her eggs in the sloth's dung, then returns to the sloth's fur.

Frog

The moist environment of the rain forest is the perfect habitat for frogs. Most lay their eggs in puddles on the ground. Some frogs live on the floor, while others climb the trees.

Emerald tree boa
The boa waits in trees to ambush birds, rodents, and even monkeys. When its prey comes close, the boa catches it with its fangs then wraps it in its coils to suffocate it.

Insects, Reptiles, and Amphibians

By sheer numbers, there are more insects than any other type of animal in the rain forest. This also means there are many animals, such as reptiles and amphibians, that eat insects as part of their diet, not to mention those predators that eat the animals that eat the insects.

Caiman
This amphibious carnivore is related to the alligator. It lurks in the water using its eyes, ears, and nose to watch for food.

Poison dart frog
This frog's bright skin says, "Go away, I'm toxic." It carries its young on its back.

Native People

For thousands of years, indigenous peoples have lived deep in the world's rain forests. Even today, millions of rain forest dwellers depend on their surroundings for food and shelter. However, when rain forests are destroyed, these people, along with many animals and plants, lose their homes and livelihoods.

Native people face tremendous pressure from the outside world, which covets the resources found in their rain forest habitats. Many find it difficult to keep their traditional, tribal ways while still having contact with the outside world.

The Chimbu
In Chimbu tribes, native to the central highlands of Papua New Guinea, the men traditionally live apart from the women and children. But today, more men live in family homes near their coffee gardens.

THE YANOMAMI

One of the largest groups of indigenous people in South America, the Yanomami maintain their traditional ways despite pressure from the modern world. Life in a Yanomami village centers around the communal house. Called a *yano*, this is a circular building made of vines and leaf thatch, with a living space in the middle.

A Yanomami child in his tribal home in Demini, Brazil

The Iban
Indigenous to the island of Borneo, the Iban traditionally live together in longhouses, structures that house connected family units.

The Mbuti
Sometimes also called pygmies, the rain forest people of the Democratic Republic of Congo live in small groups of between 15 and 60 people.

The Kayapo
The few remaining Kayapo live along the Xingu River in the Amazon. They are known to be fierce warriors and use similar land management methods, such as fertilizing soil and rotating crops, to farmers in the Western world.

Under Threat

The explosion in the world's population and the surge in technology over the past few hundred years mean that people can now easily overwhelm a rain forest that has stood for millennia. People hunger for resources found in the rain forest but do not treat them with a strong enough sense of stewardship. The result is that rain forests are under threat like never before.

Disturbing the balance

Rain forests are complex systems, with many different life-forms creating a carefully balanced web. When humans disturb that balance, the whole ecosystem is affected. A simple act, such as cutting down the tallest trees, can throw out the entire rain forest system, which may never recover.

Virgin rain forest
The untouched rain forest sustains itself in a healthy cycle of life and growth. Hundreds of years of growth, however, can be wiped out by humans in just a few days.

1 Fire Rain forests are often burned by farmers to clear the land.

2 Timber While some rain forest timber is valuable, much is not. Low-value timber is burned or turned into wood pulp.

3 Crop failure Rain forest soil is notoriously poor quality. Crops planted in it can easily fail.

4 River When there are no protective trees, water rushes into the river, taking the soil with it.

5 Palm oil Commercial plantations replace the rain forest, growing money crops, such as palm oil.

Farming
Farmers plant their crops in nutrient-poor soils. The soils degrade quickly and, after a year or two, can no longer support farming.

Timber
Clear-felled trees litter the ground. Over time, they decay, releasing their stored carbon as carbon dioxide.

1

3

2

Clearing the land
Roots, stumps, and undergrowth are burned to clear the land after the trees are cut down. This also releases stored carbon as carbon dioxide.

Benefits

R ain forests have half of the world's plant species crammed into less than 7 percent of Earth's total land. Many of these plants are a treasure trove of food and medicine sources, some of which are familiar, and some of which are waiting to be discovered. This is one of the most compelling reasons for protecting rain forests. Who knows what secrets lurk there, waiting to help people in a new way?

Food diversity

Humans eat only a few dozen of the 75,000 edible plants on the planet. This makes food supplies vulnerable to diseases. More than once, farms under attack from diseases in one part of the world have been saved with the help of rain forest plants from another part of the world.

Pineapples originally grew in rain forests.

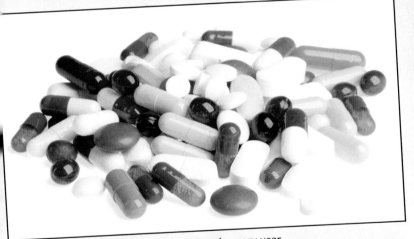

Plant-originated drugs help millions of people every year.

Rain forest medicine

Rain forest plants have been the source of one out of every four modern medicines. Plants have provided remedies for many conditions, from snake bites and poisonings to boils and headaches. Even so, less than 1 percent of all tropical plants have been tested to see if they have medical uses.

Bounty of fruits and vegetables

Plants that originated in rain forests appear on our plates every day.

The list of foods that started their lives in rain forests is surprising, both for being so long and for being so familiar. They include avocados, cashews, guavas, black pepper, coconuts, figs, citrus fruits such as oranges and lemons, bananas, corn, yams, cloves, vanilla, and chocolate. In fact, 80 percent of what people eat in the developed world first came from a rain forest somewhere.

RAIN FOREST REPORT

Miracle cure for AIDS found, then lost

In 1991, researchers found a substance in twigs from a particular Malaysian gum tree that blocked the spread of the AIDS virus in human cells. A team of biologists rushed back to Malaysia to get more, but the tree was gone. It had been cut down. No other tree has been found to have the same properties.

AIDS cure from a rain forest tree slips through researchers' hands.

7% of the world's land surface is covered by rain forest, but this number is going down. It was originally about 20 percent.

25% of all medicines used in today's modern world originated in rain forests. More are being found all the time.

28% of the world's oxygen turnover takes place in rain forest plants. This is why rain forests, such as the Amazon, are called the "lungs of the world."

40% of the rain forest canopy is made up of vines. There are more than 2,500 different vine species.

50% of the world's plant and animal species live in rain forests.

80% of the Western world's diet is plants that first came from rain forests.

88% humidity is normal in many tropical rain forests.

Rain Forest Facts

**2.5 acres (1 ha) of rain forest =
750 types of trees +
1,500 species of plants**

Rain drop rate
Rain forest plants are so dense that rain falling on the canopy can take up to 10 minutes to hit the ground.

10
9
8
7
6
5
4
3
2
1
0

Fruits
At least 3,000 varieties of fruits are found in rain forests. Only 200 are commonly eaten in the West. Indigenous people in the forests eat more than 2,000 varieties.

Insects
There are more insects in a rain forest than any other animal. For example, army ants live in colonies of up to 2 million individuals. They can easily overrun larger insects and even mammals.

Glossary

abdomen (AB-duh-mun)
The rear section of an insect or, in vertebrate animals, the stomach region.

amphibious
(am-FIH-bee-us) Living both in water and on land.

bromeliad
(bro-MEE-lee-ad) A type of epiphyte with long, stiff leaves found naturally in rain forest canopies.

canopy (KA-nuh-pee)
The portion of the rain forest that is above ground, made up mainly of the tops of trees.

carnivore (KAHR-neh-vor)
A meat-eating animal.

climate (KLY-mut)
The weather found in a particular place, over an extended period of time, indicated by factors such as temperature, rainfall, wind, and air pressure.

crown (KROWN) The top of the head.

deciduous
(deh-SIH-joo-us) Describes plants that lose their leaves seasonally.

decomposer
(dee-kum-POH-zer) An organism that causes decay in plants and animals.

degrade (dih-GRAYD)
To break down or become less rich.

diversity
(duh-VER-suh-tee) Variety.

emergent (ih-MER-jent)
Describes something that emerges or pokes out from something else.

epiphyte (EH-puh-fyt)
A plant that grows on another plant.

evergreen (EH-ver-green)
A plant or tree with leaves that remain green and functional through more than one growing season.

fungi (FUN-jy) Living organisms that include yeast, molds, mushrooms, and toadstools.

germinate
(JER-muh-nayt) To sprout or begin to grow.

indigenous
(in-DIH-jeh-nus) Native or original to a particular place.

larvae (LAHR-vee)
Immature forms of certain animals.

mammal (MA-mul)
A type of animal that has a backbone and hairy skin, suckles its young with milk, and, in most species, gives birth to live young.

monsoon (mon-SOON)
A sustained seasonal wind that often produces heavy rain, usually occurring in southern Asia.

orchid (OR-kud) A type of flowering epiphyte known for its beauty.

plumage (PLOO-mij)
A bird's feathers, including their color and pattern.

predator (PREH-duh-ter)
An animal that eats another type of animal.

primate (PRY-mayt)
A member of a group of animals that includes lemurs, monkeys, gorillas, and humans.

reptile (REP-tyl) A type of cold-blooded animal that includes lizards, snakes, turtles, and alligators.

reservoir (REH-zuh-vwar)
A storage area for water.

temperate (TEM-puh-rut)
Describes moderate weather
that does not vary too much.

termite (TUR-myt) An insect
similar to an ant, which
eats wood.

vegetation (veh-jih-TAY-shun)
All plant life.

vine (VYN) A type of plant that
supports itself by climbing,
twining, or creeping on something
else, rather than supporting itself
using its stem.

Index

Websites

Due to the changing nature of Internet links, PowerKids Press has developed an online list of websites related to the subject of this book. This site is updated regularly. Please use this link to access the list: www.powerkidslinks.com/disc/rain/